Date: 8/17/18

BR COAN
Coan, Sharon,
Big Pig /

Big Pig

Consultants

Ashley Bishop, Ed.D.

Sue Bishop, M.E.D.

Publishing Credits

Dona Herweck Rice, *Editor-in-Chief*

Robin Erickson, *Production Director*

Lee Aucoin, *Creative Director*

Tim J. Bradley, *Illustrator Manager*

Jason Peltz, *Illustrator*

Sharon Coan, *Project Manager*

Jamey Acosta, *Editor*

Rachelle Cracchiolo, M.A.Ed., *Publisher*

Teacher Created Materials

5301 Oceanus Drive
Huntington Beach, CA 92649-1030
http://www.tcmpub.com

ISBN 978-1-4333-2929-6

© 2012 Teacher Created Materials, Inc.

pig

He is a pig.

big

He is big.

dig

He can dig.

wig

He has a wig.

He can jig!

Glossary

big

dig

jig

pig

wig

Sight Words

He   is

a   can

has

Extension Activities

Read the story together with your child. Use the discussion questions before, during, and after your reading to deepen your child's understanding of the story and the rime (word family) that is introduced.

The activities provide fun ideas for continuing the conversation about the story and the vocabulary that is introduced. They will help your child make personal connections to the story and use the vocabulary to describe prior experiences.

Discussion Questions

- How can you tell that the pig is big? What other animals can you think of that are big?

- Why does the pig dig? What other animals dig?

- Have you ever seen a wig? Who wears wigs?

- Would you like to visit a farm with animals that can do silly things? Why or why not?

Activities at Home

- Find big things around your house and have your child use the following sentence frame to talk about them: "The _____ is big." With each big item, review the *-ig* rime.

- Work together to write questions that can be answered using the phrases in the story. For example, your child may help you write the following question: "Who can dig?" Together, you and your child may say and/or write an appropriate answer: "The pig can dig."